T0132462

The Unfairness Of Angels

The Unfairness Of Angels

by Matthew Bartram

iUniverse, Inc.
New York   Bloomington

The Unfairness Of Angels

Copyright © 2010 by Matthew Bartram

All rights reserved. No part of this book may be used or reproduced by any means, graphic, electronic, or mechanical, including photocopying, recording, taping or by any information storage retrieval system without the written permission of the publisher except in the case of brief quotations embodied in critical articles and reviews.

The views expressed in this work are solely those of the author and do not necessarily reflect the views of the publisher, and the publisher hereby disclaims any responsibility for them.

iUniverse books may be ordered through booksellers or by contacting:

iUniverse
1663 Liberty Drive
Bloomington, IN 47403
www.iuniverse.com
1-800-Authors (1-800-288-4677)

Because of the dynamic nature of the Internet, any Web addresses or links contained in this book may have changed since publication and may no longer be valid.

Front cover photo by Matthew Bartram

ISBN: 978-1-4401-9999-8 (sc)
ISBN: 978-1-4502-0000-4 (dj)
ISBN: 978-1-4502-0111-7 (ebk)

Printed in the United States of America

iUniverse rev. date: 1/27/2010

For Mum:

Joyce Lewis

Always And Forever In My Thoughts:

Dedication:

My Mum died on February 28th 2006. I held her hand as she passed into another realm. She is much missed and always loved. I dedicate this book to my Mum, who was the most amazing woman I have ever met. I am honoured to have had her, not only as my Mum, but also as a teacher of life. She taught my brothers and I all about morality, values, friendships and how important it was to be a family. She lived for us and we lived for her. Her teachings will live on in my brothers, their children, in me, and of course, in this book of poetry.

Contents

Introduction

In July 2005, my Mum was diagnosed with bowel cancer - she was 59 years old. In November of that year, she was going to turn 60, a milestone in any person's life. Yet this was one life that might not reach another celebration. So I decided to write her a poetry book, a unique gift for a unique person.

My mum died a few months after her 60th birthday - her book still takes pride of place on my bookshelf. In 2009, I decided to rewrite Mum's book to add some old and new poems spanning my whole poetry life. This is the book you are about to read: The Unfairness of Angels, an eternal memory to my mum, as well a rollercoaster ride of my emotions and stories and snapshots of England and contemporary life, love, theology and morality.

So please join me on this moving journey, through my misdemeanours and adventures as I seek to answer life's many questions and discover the Unfairness of Angels

Joyce Welstead

You were born Joyce Dorothy Welstead,
You didn't know what was ahead.
Youngest of three, two brothers you had
Dorothy your Mum, Thomas your Dad.
Born in London, just like me.
You truly were just lovely.
You lived in Ealing, born and bred
You had frizzy hair on your head.
It was hair that was your trade,
As a hairdresser you were paid.
I've seen the photos of you at school,
And you really were beautiful.
Good looks and a warm heart,
Sometimes, I don't know where to start.

You met Dad when he was working in a shop,
And love must have hit the spot.
You settled down and had a son,
David was number one.
Soon came along number two,
That's me, your poet, Matthew!
Joyce, David, Matthew and my Dad, Ken
But then I had another brother, Ben.
We were such a close family,
And you gave your love so freely.
I was a sick child and you took care of me,
You gave us all a wonderful memory.
You continued to cut hair, but went alone,
Cutting hair in our home.

Your laughter was heard everywhere,
It was joyful and free to share.
You taught us manners and morals too -
And what was false and what was true!
We moved then to Midhurst Road,
But we never moved our family code.
Be honest, be yourself, love is free.
Well, it was in our family.
When Dad left and we were minus one,
You became a Dad and a Mum.
Here is when I saw you grow,
From width to length.
You were our tower of strength!
Times were hard back then,
Bailiffs coming, but we never knew when.

You held us all together
We became fighters and we never said never!
Your reward for being so brave,
Was finding love with Dave.
You brought him, like your boys,
Happiness and joy of joys.
And when life was treating us just right,
You suddenly had to fight,
An illness that brings misery,
Not to just our family.
And in the darkest, darkest time,
You still were in your prime.
When death was passed onto you,
You said, "You alright Matthew?"
Thinking of me when you were sick,
I will never, ever forget it!
Those last few months, were not you,
Physically weak, but your love still true.
Then it came to pass, with you by my side,
We said our last goodbyes.

Mother

A protective force,
A loving friend.
A warming glow,
An endless trend.

Forever within our minds,
Forever gentle,
Forever kind.
The woman with us -
From life to death,
She gave us our first breath.

Always helping throughout life,
With all the hard and troubled strife.
Mum, I admit that it's true,
There's no other I love -
But you.

Brave And Strong

Letting go of your hand, I saw you drift away.
Filled with tears, I found it hard to say;
How much I'll miss,
My goodnight kiss.

Just having you around, knowing you were there,
I think these things, as I look and stare.
I thought about you when I travelled over sea,
About the one person that has made me, me.

I see the wires coming from your nose and arms...
And the red corded nurse alarms.
I can't believe, less than a year ago, you were well,
Then cancer got you and brought us all to hell!

But you never complained, you just soldiered on,
Because you're my Mum, brave and strong!
Every tear I shed, another quickly comes again
I hate this bastard cancer, the bringer of pain!

They can send men to space and make mobile phones,
But can do nothing to stop this destroyer of homes
I won't change from the person I am, you see,
You have created my destiny.

I will be brave and strong and kind too -
And by doing so, I'll be just like you.

The Emotional Rock

I cried today, within the busy streets of London,
It was a windy day and tears were streaming down my face,
Merging with my runny nose and sniffling.
Just another Englishman putting up with the weather.
But my emotions were running wild,
It was the day before Mothers Day...
Except Mothers Day is every day to me.

Recently I've been having flashbacks of a past memory,
I was a small boy, blonde haired and full of life...
I went to live with a couple called Jenny and Graham,
I only found out later it was because
Mum and Dad had problems.
He had spent all the money we never had -
Ran up huge debts, he was living another life.
Hard to have both, children and a wife

My Mum's parents sold their house -
To pay off his debts. This was going on
Whilst I sat under a tree with my brother,
Listening to Michael Jackson's
Thriller album on his Walkman.

I remember the comfort of strangers.
Soft words and a gentle presence.
Years went on and my Dad did it again,
This time there was no money to bail us out.

I was at school, older brother away, little brother at home,
I lived on handouts from friends and free school meals -
As everyone around me had everything they wanted.
I had nothing. I went to college with a heart full of sorrow,
Every day I came home,
Not knowing if I would be here tomorrow?

I went to University, a working class warrior.
I was sent to live in a council estate on the top floor
Looking over London's scum.
But, Mum met Dave and he helped us out-
Sold everything he had to help Mum...
They got married and they lived like a King and Queen.

With nothing, I had come a long way
I've travelled the world twice!
With money I saved for over two years!
I've climbed life's ladder,
With nothing but hard work and constant battles.
But today, this afternoon,
I had memories, so many in one blast
About the past...

A sick and clumsy child I was,
Could not read or write, or speak properly,
Bad eyesight, tongue tied, I went from Doctor to Doctor.
Despite all this, I was always happy.
I fill up now, tears will follow.

At 16, I was found to be dyslexic.
Not the stupid lazy child,
The teachers thought I was.

Tears at the edge of my eyes,
While I write this -
Wanting to stream down my face...

I hear everyone around me,
Say nice things about me,
Amazing man, so warm, so kind, so loving…And I am,
Although so many people have tried to hurt me -
Inject poisonous thoughts and hate into me…
But I cannot hate for long…
I was brought up to know what's right and wrong.

Only one person is to thank for this…
Only one person, has made me the person..
You like!
An eternal Goddess has
Created the person I am today
This person, is my Mother!
My Mum, someone who I love beyond love.

And today, when I bought her -
A Mothers Day card…
I realised, material gifts mean nothing.
The love I have for my Mum, is priceless.

And now Mum's sick and our world is rocked again…
But with love and memories, our world will be defiant -
With a soul, a heart and a smile, nothing can conquer us,
For you are my soul and my heart and my smile…

My emotional rock.

Drops Of Blood

I had a dream about drops of blood falling
Over a cliff - falling, forever, before a sudden
Impact! Watching the blood fall into the abyss below;
Tasting the blood upon my breath...
I realised, I was dreaming of death!

I awoke to find my chest and face covered
In blood; I had an operation a few days before
On my nose...I was told if it started to bleed, to go
To a hospital. Non-stop; it poured drops
Of blood...Panic set in and then fear!

Fear has a colour, I now know. It is
White, a bright, ashen white, my face
Had gone a pale shade of winter. Running
Into the bathroom, I catch a glimpse of the midnight
Hour: water runs from taps, like my blood. My pain
Is riddled with fear!

Head pounding, stomach sick with
Blood's aroma - Brother asleep
With his girlfriend...Mum asleep downstairs...
But I am not coping
Not coping at all!

With my hands resembling a murderer -
I go downstairs to the bathroom
And call for Mum. Like the angel she is,
She appears. Sits me down, and attends
To my nosebleed. Reassuring me, telling me
Not to panic…Stories she tells of when
I was a little boy. Nosebleeds I used to have,
I feel like a boy now…Scared, frightened
Everything will be OK now,
Because Mum's here,
Time went slowly, but the blood
Eased, as did my fear.

I returned to my bed…
To dream about drops of blood!

I Remember

I remember my first day at school,
Running down the corridors,
Not wanting you to leave
At all.

I remember when I had bad dreams,
And Dad was always the monster...
But you showed me, not everything
Is what it seems.

I remember our holidays with the family
Down in Devon, Cornwall and Majorca...
And me crying all the way home
Missing a donkey.

I remember when I was sick and ill -
And you being with me always...
Like you are
Still.

There is so much I remember!
I'm sure you do too, Mum,
Like when you gave birth to me
On the 16th of September.

A Mother's Wisdom

Walking back from work
Down by the canal
Towards my home -
October's winter sunset
Shining, like a king upon his throne.
It's shimmering light casts
Upon the canal's murky waters…

I have flashbacks
About what you taught us..
Be good, behave and always remember
To say please!
And to say bless you
When you sneeze…
Images of youth bring a smile
To my face, as I walk silently home,
Staring into space.

The sky gets darker and I see
The wishing star in the sky…
So, I close my eyes really hard
And make a wish…
For you to be well.

Faces In The Mist

If words could come to life
I'd spell out your name.
Mother and wife
Equal love the same.

Three years have now gone,
But you're still missed,
But there's nothing wrong,
In seeing faces in the mist.

You left when things were good,
And missed our fall from grace.
Lost in the deepest wood,
In a darkened place.

But now time has healed,
No traces of where you kissed.
Our lives we slowly build,
Amongst the faces in the mist.

Weep we still do,
Not so much any more.
Yet we always think of you,
This, we can't ignore.

Slowly we move on,
Ticking things off our list.
Always seeing you,
In the faces in the mist.

Dear Mr Christ

'Dear Mr Christ,

Please allow me to introduce myself to you.
My name is Matthew.
I'll admit I don't believe what the Bible says is true.
As a man, I am sure you did exist.
But as a God? Or Son of God? I don't believe this.
I heard you have healing and amazing powers?
So why not use them when those planes hit the Towers?
And that recent earthquake in Pakistan?
And the evil which seems to stem from Man?
And let us not ignore…Every, single, bloody war!
Let's say, we give you the benefit of the doubt,
Could you not have helped Africa with its drought?

I hear people talk about free will and natural disasters,
But why treat us like bastards?
Did you know that all these murderers, rapists and thieves,
Think that you will help them through your beliefs?
This makes you just as guilty as them!
We are created in your own image then?
Did you know that my Mum believed in you?
Even went to church too…
But throughout her life, you never believed in her.
And for that, I will never forgive you Sir…

I saw how upset she was when my Dad did what he did,
And I saw you, in the shadows so concisely hid…
I believe, you're just a figment of Man's imagination,
Created to burden our frustration.
An imaginary friend built from our dreams,
Falling apart from the seams.
Let me explain something, my Mum means the world to me,
So I want you to try and see…
That although I don't believe in you,
I was wondering if there's anything you could do?
As a historical figure, I think you were superb,
But anything else is simply absurd!
I know Heaven is supposed to be nice for eternity,
But I really don't think it is for me.
I believe in what I know, my friends and family.
Well it's late here and I really have to go
But I'm asking for your help
As you just never know?
What is fiction and what is true?

Yours Sincerely
Matthew

When The Weeping Seems To Start

Slowly, gently
I feel you brush
Against me.
Calming, warming,
You come without a warning.
I wish you were with us,
I can't foresee the triggers
But, when I feel you in my heart,
Is when the weeping seems to start.

My grief becomes anger!
I feel I've betrayed her,
I become weak,
When I should be strong!
Sometimes, you find answers
Being wrong.

The long path has been
Sodden,
But memories are never
Forgotten - we never did part,
Thinking makes the weeping start.

I want to show you what's new,
And tell you
I love you!
I have only photos to show
People who you know,
How I made you
Proud,
My silence seems so
Loud.

The empty feeling seems
So numb,
That is when I weep
Mum .
Upon my soul you hang,
Like my favourite piece of art.
Then the weeping seems to start.

Thank You

As a man, I will never be able to feel
The magic of giving birth.
And see what was a part of me,
Grow into a man and walk this earth.
I hold my hands up and accept this will never be,
This is one thing these eyes will never see.
I'll never be able to call myself Mum.
But I can say thank you to a special someone.
Someone who bore me, and made me feel real.
This person is the real deal.
I'll never forget you,
And I'll never stop loving you…
Sometimes, the simple words say it all,
So I would like to say; "Thank you."

She

She gave a glow and warmth,
Like a cosy fire burning,
In a homely cottage
With snow outside on the moors.
Yet inside, you're snug and safe.

She filled you like a jug of wine,
Always keeping your glass full,
Enriching you with a rich fruity
Full-bodied feeling.
Empowered by mirth.

She was the face everyone knew,
Making you smile
Stopping in the street to chat,
Idle gossip, but always
Proud of her boys.

She was as wise as Yoda ,
And as compassionate as
Florence Nightingale.
Tending her gallant brave soldiers,
Back from society's Wars.

She was our Mum,
Wife and Sister,
Daughter
And Grandmother,
In Heaven.

I Kissed The Lines On Your Beautiful Face

I was driving my car to work this morning,
Yes Mum, I now drive, how worrying.
And whilst waiting by the lights at Brentford,
Just by the station, your voice I heard.

And for a brief second, I had a flashback,
And my heart sank as I wanted you back.
The beep of the horn behind me
Brought me back to reality.

But for that second, I was lost in space,
I kissed the lines on your beautiful face.
I now live alone, in the house, number 4,
And although I have Maurice, I cannot ignore.

The pictures, the photos, and the plates on the wall -
I remember a time when we had it all.
The parties, the Christmases, a house full of fun,
Never did I think I'd be the last one.

And although I know I'll be fine,
I often get trapped in a zone, with no time.
And for that split second, I'm lost in space,
I kiss the lines on your beautiful face.

I remember kissing those lines on your beautiful face,
As I wipe the tears, with fingers I trace,
Feeling the need to gently grace,
The lines which are yours, on my beautiful face.

Sunday Roast

Amazing what we take for granted,
Is what we miss the most.
And now that we have parted,
I miss your Sunday Roast.

I miss the way every Sunday
We were all around the table.
Time for the whole family,
To discuss a little fable.

The way you cooked that chicken,
And the golden roast potatoes.
This is what I am missing,
And in my heart it shows.

So many "thank you's" I wish I'd said,
Amongst the gravy and ginger beer.
The way the vegetables were spread
And the sound of friendly cheer.

I used to come back muddy,
From playing football with my mate.
But 6pm every Sunday,
I had the best dinner on my plate.

Now you are gone,
I have beans on toast,
And although the odd one comes along,
I miss your Sunday roast.

Noah and the Golden Age

The other day I visited my brother for a barbecue,
And met Noah, my gorgeous little nephew.
It had been a while since I'd seen him,
And in that time, he'd done some growing.
After the cuddles and the playing with toys,
He went out for walk, with the Bartram Boys.
Three generations of Bartrams all together,
Me, my Dad, and my little and older brother.
Behind my brother's house is beautiful countryside,
Noah brought his bike to ride,
Well he doesn't ride, we push him!
And it started me thinking,
What world will this little man grow into?
What technology will become new?
When I was a boy, we had no mobile phones!
And no computers in our homes!
Will QPR be a better football team?
Will he still be able to drink alcohol at eighteen?
Will he be able to have a bet?
And what will happen to the internet?
Will he be like his uncles or his Daddy?
Will he write poetry?
Will he have a sister or another brother?
I will tell him stories about his Grandmother,
I get sad when I think that Mum will never see him,
At least he didn't have to hear her sing!
Sorry Mum, 'love you', only joking.
Will he still put rubbish in a bin?
Whatever happens, it will be challenging,
I just hope he does what I did and go travelling.
I hope he will have a niece or a nephew,

Especially from his Uncle Matthew!
And then my brothers start talking to me,
And bring me back to reality.
The joys of being a family!
One thing he will learn from Uncle Matty
Is being the master of the poetic page!
'Noah and the Golden Age.'

Your Grandmother

Today in my garden,
Whilst the bumblebee suckled upon the pollen.
I told you of a person, who you won't see -
But is never forgotten.

And as you reached out
To grasp the yellow buttered dandelion.
I whispered in your ear -
About another time,

About this amazing goddess,
And precious lady.
Who, if she were around
Today would spoil you crazy.

Your big, beautiful
Ocean-blue eyes.
Just answered me back,
With a baby's cries.

I held you and kissed
Your soft cheeks . And I told you-
About where I'd been
These past weeks.

About my journeys
To distant lands.
I looked at your little grip,
In my hands.

And the warm summer breeze,
Brushed against us - and I cuddled you,
Close to me,
Without any fuss

Maurice came over the shed
And into the garden
And you burped in my ear,
And I said "pardon."

Such innocence within a time of change,
But my little nephew,
You will soon find this world,
So strange

But with love and honesty - and a strong,
And caring family, you will know
Of the greatest memory - like no other.
When I will tell you, about my Mother.
And how she still spoils you and loves you, little Noah.

Down The Snow-Tale Path

Guided not only by the hand of nature,
But of love and knowledge. Down a path
Which only yesterday was firm,
Like the grip you now hold.

Forced to wear plastic boots on the wet sodden soil.
Past the bare trees, now sprinkled with white,
Snow lays on the green grass - the fresh air
And cold chill brings a rosy colour to your cheeks.

The full wonderment of nature,
Surrounds you - guides you.
The giant beside you talks words,
Of muffled sounds.

Through your woolly bobbled hat,
Your eyes, like your mind, are focused.
Like oval sapphire gems on white clouds,
Floating in all directions.

You make noises to communicate,
Short, sharp thrills of joy.
As those little legs -
go a-walking down the snow-tale path.

Bottom Of The Sea

I once knew a place, at the bottom of the sea,
Cold, dark, desolate and empty.
Endless, yet claustrophobic,
Arms flapping, but nothing to grip,
Every part of me, moved slowly,
Suffocating and empty,
There's no further to fall,
You feel the currents pull,
Oxygen fading, time to make a choice.
From above, you hear a voice,
A voice, so full of life and hope,
At last, you're given some rope!
Legs swing systematically into motion,
Soon, you're not alone in the ocean.
You prepare to face the bends,
But it's worth it, to be with friends,
Soon you see life again,
Coral reefs and the beauty of the sea,
Those sharks are now graceful fish,
Not from your nightmare list.
You'll never forget that feeling,
And your lifeless soul screaming.
Eventually, you see the sky
And a boat passing by,
A local fishing boat
Sees you afloat,
A hand pulls you aboard,
Mightier than the Lord,
Voices cheer all around,
Been so long since you've heard that sound.
They wrap you up and feed your stomach,
You can't believe how much you fucked up.
The boat takes you back to land,
Rock Bottom's a place, you now understand!

The Real Five Horsemen

Alone,
Within an abyss of darkness
You stumble,
Upon a clattering of rocks!
Bare feet, cut, bloody and
Sore - bending down, you reach into
Nothingness - you feel first
One, then two, sharp rocks.
As you bang them together - a spark
Arrives giving a glimpse of dried leaves.
Scrambling over, you touch them - smashing
The rocks together, sparks fly - until
The leaves become a fire, a light,
A beacon within this darkest
And most terrible place -
You realise, there is
Hope!

How easy it is to mistake hate for hurt -
And allow past feelings to send you berserk.
Thinking about the injustice of past actions –
Erasing the memory of past infatuations.

It's like drinking hot acid,
That sticks in your chest…
Making your stomach tie up
in knots! It lingers, for days,
Until it reaches your mind.
You question the morality
Of humankind.
Like eating sandwiches with metal in -
You feel heavy inside
You're suffering.
Images and thoughts plague your daily routine.
You think it was all
A dream. It takes years, maybe
A lifetime to get rid of it.
On good days you feel like
Shit!
Then the parasite that did this
To you… infects you with
Hurt.

My blood-stained sword, talks of,
Judgement.
Rendering vengeance
On my enemies.
I repay those who hated me -
With arrows dunked in poison
My sword
Will devour flesh,
My anger
Will cause a bloody flood!
I will rip down
Forests with my gauntlet of pain.
My anger
Has subsided -
Nothing will be the same.
As the sound of
Steel and
Bone meet - **Vengeance!**

A flower's
Petals shaped like hearts,
Red in colour,
Stem is strong,
Slim, sublime.
Roots dig deep
Into salvation,
Integrating within the
Earth…the hot sun feeds you -
Tears of rain
Come down…
Quenching natural
Beauty.
Everyday you grow
Into a single word -
Perfection.

The Suicidal Orange

I'm the Orange, feeling suicidal,
I just want to end it all,
It's really unfair -
He should be called green, not pear!

No wonder I'm suicidal,
Sitting next to the apple -
Please don't tell me it's fate!
That they called him grape.

Why isn't the banana called yellow?
That's what I want to know!
In schools what do they teach?
Are they biased towards the peach?

And what about the Kiwi?
That should be called 'small and prickly'!
It's not just fruit, but the vegetable,
This makes me different and suicidal.

The more I see, the more I get down,
Why isn't the potato called brown?
Sometimes, I get so upset I can't speak,
You've got a cool name, don't you, Leek!

Then there's cabbage and lettuce too!
Blueberries should be called 'blue'!
It's unfair and it makes me mad!
No wonder I am always sad.

I have issues from when I was young,
They squashed my Dad and Mum.
My brothers and sisters went to Spain,
And I never saw them again.

I found a friend in Cocktails,
Turned to vodka when I went off the rails.
I needed to blank out my pain.
Orange is not my real name.

Orange is such an ugly colour,
They could have chosen another?
I have the most boring, unoriginal name,
I was actually christened…Shane!

Humans In A Fish Bowl

Tap! Tap! Tap!

Is the sound I make,
When I come to the end of my world.
Glass in front of me, the mountain blocks
My vision of freedom. I see
The path I must take.
I believe the grass is always greener.

My face squashed, my hands touch
An invisible screen

Tap! Tap! Tap!

Making a tinning noise
Like hitting a spoon against a wine glass,
When you're about to make a great speech.

Tap! Tap! Tap!

I turn around and I see the sun setting-
Clouds like a dragon's flame.
Sky, like an erupting volcano!

The only sound I hear is of me
Trying to escape
To wonder…

Emotions cramp my stomach,
Fear of the unknown!
And the realisation that we
Don't live in a real world!
I see reality
A millimetre in front of me.

Tap! Tap!
Tap!

A human in a fish bowl.

Bowling With Convicts

I took a bunch of ex-cons bowling today,
I do social work a different way…
At the bowling alley, it was Pete's turn to begin,
He said, the only alley he knew was the one he slept in!
Jack told of the time he *'shot up smack.'*
Whilst Dave bowled, talking about crack.
Robin said he dealt inside prison without a care,
Then smiled, when he got a spare.
Jack said he got five years for attacking a man with a spike
Then jumped for joy when he got a strike.
Barry said his life was shooting up in McDonalds loos,
He then looked for more bowls, and asked *"where's the blues?"*
I told him I would go and get one for him;
Jack continued his story, *"the fool needed it! He nicked my gin!"*
Raj said he was having a bad week
Whereas Sam just bowled his game and didn't speak.
Funny, seeing such hard men play this game…
Deep inside, they feel the shame
There's a couple bowling, next row down…
Never know, he might've been sent down?
After the bowling, we all went for a Chinese,
They were very polite, saying *thank you,* and *please*
Muscat, as he was known to the guys;
Was saying how he got off *'scot free',* with a string of lies.
Raj was still feeling rather sad
So I took him aside and he told me about his Dad…

Dying in the local Hospital down the road,
Like father, like son, no fixed abode!
I told him he was free to leave, I would not inform parole,
I look round: Jack was still on a roll!
There were a lot of good feelings around
They all thanked me, and said I was sound.
After the meal, they all went their separate ways...
Promising to keep to our next appointment,
joking; it was at Safeways!
On the train back home that night; for dinner with Mother
I realised you can't judge a book by its cover,
And although society sees them as little shits!
Nothing beats bowling, with convicts.

Drug Stories

From the gay crack head, injecting into his penis!
Even though he doesn't get paid, for that intravenous.
The 18 year old homeless girl
Living with a punter with greying hair,
Just hoping that the price is fair.
The 40 year old first timer on brown;
Stole for a fix and now she's going down!
The beaten housewife who pops pills
The crack house landlords…Conducting business
From under the floorboards!
The mother's baby who's addicted to heroin!
The young child with AIDS, an abandoned needle
Found in the bin!
The homeless, the working and middle class,
The young boy, getting paid in crack
For sex up the arse!
The ex-prisoners, just let out of the nick,
With a new heroin habit!
Can't afford real society's prices - soon
End up a homeless crisis!
Men and women, boys and girls,
All wanting to go straight
But another pill, shot, smoke of the pipe
And it's all too late!
All the things they might have been.
No work, no future and no home!
Drugs stories, published by, methadone!

Another Slap

"You're late, where have you been?
What men have you seen?
Another dinner date? With that man Ross!
Don't give me that shit about him being your boss!
Look at you, all dressed up like some slag!
With your make-up on and your designer handbag!
I don't bloody work to make you look like a tart!
Now go and make my dinner before the football starts!
Did I tell you to answer me back?
Do you really want another slap?"

"In future, you dress like a woman and behave like one!
I can't have my friends thinking I married scum!
What, you still here?
Fuck off! And get me a beer!
I can hear you on your mobile phone!
You're never going out, you're staying home!
And stop that crying!
You sound like a cat dying!
I said, stop that!
Do you really want another slap?"

"Hurry up with the dinner!
I am meeting my friends at eight!
Will you stop crying and acting a state!
Stop bloody crying! Are you deaf as well as dumb?
And stop talking about me to your Mum!
I know you've been talking to her about our row!
Your Mum's a bitch; a stupid cow!
Just like you as a matter of fact!
Do you really want another slap?"

"Don't come in here, crying to me!
And put that knife down, it makes you look silly!
I said, put that knife down! You stupid slag!
And stop crying! You lost your rag?
Put that knife down! Now!"

"What the hell
Do you think you're doing? You stupid cow!
Arrgh! You bloody bitch! That hurt!
Do you want more blood on your skirt?
Arrgh! Arrgh! Stop! Arrgh! Please!
Arrgh! I was only joking, only being a tease.
Arrrrrgh! I think I am bleeding from my heart?
Listen, let's call it quits and make a new start.
I…Arrrgh! I love you. You know that?
You're killing me, you bitch!
You want another slap?"

The Prisoner Poet

On an island, surrounded by a stormy sea
I live in a prison, sentenced, for eternity!
My hair's long, matted and grey
My soul longs to be set free one day.
I'm so skinny and frail, I can see my veins!
I sleep on a bed, that is covered in stains.
I live in a tower, in a room so small.
I deserve what I got, for a life so cruel!

I've been compared to a living nightmare
In the past, I've done crimes without a care.
I've been here, in my own personal hell.
And I've only just started my prison spell.
I've kept my head down and caused no harm,
Polite to the guards, I put on the charm,
Rewarded with a desk, chair, paper and a pen...
I could have more, but they didn't say when.

I sit here and write poetry, verses so beautiful,
About a life I wish I had, when I was small.
I write and I write, my pen just flows,
Writing poetry, stories and of course prose.
Yet, I am a man hated in society.
I can't undo the pain I've caused, or the misery.
So I sit and write, poem after poem for no-one;
Words so beautifully written by scum.

The paper stacks up on my desk
And the guards read some,
They know, about the crimes I've done.
I overheard one of the guards say one night…
About a row they had with their wife, some silly fight.
He remembered a poem of mine he read.
He told his wife the poem and they ended up in bed.
She told him it was the
Most amazing, heartfelt poem she'd heard;
She asked him if he wrote it? He said;
"No, just some guy doing the bird."

Through words, I create myself a new life;
Poems that can charm the guard's wife!
I write in a world where I'm the King;
And all my crimes don't mean a thing!
I create my own justice and fair trial!
Where people don't grimace, but only smile.
I write my poems both day and night
With each stroke of the pen and word I write.
Confined to my cell, in my world full of shit!
Lives a guilty man,
Who is a prisoner poet!

The Black Mile

The day came, I've waited a long time,
I had plenty of reflecting to do, upon my crime.
The guard asked me for my last meal,
I didn't really give a fuck, as it was no big deal.

I asked for fish and chips,
I heard a muttering under his lips.
I had been waiting for Death Row, for a few years,
Don't worry, it's OK, I shed no tears.

I laugh, my mind they thought they could treat
I told them, I would kill again,
There was no deceit.
The doctors said, 'I was not mentally insane!'
Just 'pure evil' and 'enjoyed others pain'

The door opened and a plate was pushed through the gap,
At least I don't have to eat any more of this crap!
The guard looked at me; "Why did you
kill those girls?" He said,
I shrugged, "just wanted to see what they looked like dead."
He looked at me and spat in my cell!
"You sick evil bastard! Go to hell!"
"Don't believe in it!" I told him.

I've killed so many women!
I remember the first one
I don't know what she'd done?
I guess it was creative art,
I do after all have a heart!

The image of her choking to death
And her grasping for a final breath,
I became addicted, you see,
I think I murdered about 33?

Four big guards came to collect me,
I told them I'll come freely.
see how nice I am really?
I passed Tommy in cell four,
He was my friend,
But I guess all killing must come to an end?
Tommy was going to be executed next Monday,
He told me he killed men who were gay.

The long walk wasn't as bad as I thought,
My only regret was that I got caught,
I go into this room, it's a full house!
I think of that film *"The Green Mile"* and Mr Jingles the mouse
I see weeping women and angry men,
And a little boy about ten?

He shouts that I killed his Mummy!
I smile, I find it all so funny.
The leather straps are tied onto my arms
As I sit in the chair. They put wires on me,
And then shave my hair!
I liked my hair long
I think that's wrong!
I didn't come here for a haircut
Christ Almighty, I only killed some slut!

They put this thing on my head
In thirty seconds I'll be dead!
I manage to lift my middle finger to the boy,
I manage a smile, I am here to destroy!

The seconds begin to tick…
I then start to kick
The pain is minimal,
I am a lucky criminal!

Neil Young's Rehab

In my cold fever, I lay in my bedsit, wondering what I've done?
It seemed appropriate that I was listening, to Neil Young.
'I've seen the needle and the damage done!'
As the fever grips me, I realize I have succumbed!
Started with a fag, a puff and a can of cider,
But as society became tougher, my drugs became harder.
I met this girl and a few friends that liked me…
But I guess not that much, as they stole my money.
They introduced me to the wilder side of drugs,
I remember the days, crashing out on hot rock rugs,
Drifting off to the sound of *'Paint It Black'*
That's how I got the taste for my buddy, smack
And his evil twin brother crack
Now there was no turning back!
I worked once as a car mechanic,
But all I fix now is me!
Through the syringe, I accept my destiny.
I had a girlfriend, a house, a car
And really good friends
Now all I've got is a mind that bends!
I lost my job, lost my wife
Between the sheets.
I've stolen for greed, and
Begged on the streets!
Somehow, I don't remember when?
I rediscovered my faith in men,
I was offered support
From a woman called Jen.
A drop-in centre,
I've never been before
I was at my lowest ebb,

My arms were so sore.
They didn't want to turn me in...
They didn't see what I did was sin!
I told them my name was Lee...
They said they'd help me.
A few months have gone by,
And I have reduced my intake,
I am not off drugs. I'm not a fake!
But I see a light
At the end of the road...
I am no longer classed as
no fixed abode!
I now listen to
Neil Young's
Harvest Moon
As I know
I will be off
Drugs soon...
Now when I hear;
'The Needle
and the
Damage Done!'
I understand it can happen to anyone.

The Loneliness Of The Long Distance Lorry Driver

Minutes seem like hours, hours seem like days,
As I drive up and down the motorways.
I'm the hidden gem of the economy.
I deliver your goods, for your shopping spree,
From timber, to tyres, coffee to cane,
You pass me by, on the fast lane.
Up and down the M1,
Never stopping till my job is done.

Just my thoughts and the radio
I venture into towns, come sun or snow.
I think about my wife and my other loves,
As I add another cigarette to the pile of stubs.
Through rainstorms and rainbows…
I go up and down so many roads.

Not knowing what's in the back of my truck,
I just sign the forms and pray for luck!
Headlight beams from the passing traffic,
Spellbind me into something magic.
Of dreams and visions of what might have been?
The beeping horn reminds me, it's just a dream.

Through Patrick Gilmore's Eyes

No real reasons why or given?
Sometimes, we're just not that driven.
Each knock, each setback builds!
Leaving dents in our human shields;
Dents that that leave a devastating amount,
Like a sinking bank account
So, no! I don't know why?
Another young soul has to die.
But die you did and now you're gone,
But in this life, you did nothing wrong

I remember you at school,
And playing five-a-side football.
Coming round my house with the guys,
And getting drunk, which is no surprise!
I remember us meeting in Hungary
Me, you and Johnny P,
Running away from the cops in Budapest,
Hiding in a club to escape arrest.
And then you went to Vietnam,
And dazzled the ladies with your charm.

But I guess, the drugs and the alcohol
In the end took it's toll?
Escaping what? We'll never know,
But now my friend, you've left the show!
Curtains drawn, applause is heard,
"Come back!" we cry, but that's absurd .
Because you're not coming back,
You've slipped through the crack
Onto another adventure, another tale…
So goodbye my friend, and farewell!

Image

Fat,
Bald,
Short or
Tall!
Shouting;

"Mirror, mirror, on the wall!"

Reading magazines,
Watching television
Forcing us into
manic depression!

West is the best
Must be like the rest!
Tone up,
Slim down
Can't look ugly
In your gown!

Facial scrubs...
In fancy bathtubs
Let's dress up
Our girls
In little pigtails!
And plastic
Muscle men toys!
Make them into
Army boys,

Music industry pumps
Out shit!
So sexy girls
Can get a hit!
Let's advertise
Drink
With slim
Models in pink
And promote cars...
With hard man scars!

Yet all the time this takes place
The teenager thinks
About the spot on her face!
Her bulging waistline...
Which is actually
Fine!
She can't get relationships, because
She's got chapped lips!

The boy who never wins - and the men with double chins
The beer-bellied man, buying the Slim Action Plan!
Marketing kills - overpriced slimming pills!
Yet as another young girl thinks the same
Another person feels the pain.

Alternative Bob Dylan

How many pies must a man eat, before you call him obese?
The answer my friend, is in his grease!
And how many times must a man tell his lies?
The answer my friend, is between his thighs!
And how many books must a man read, before he's omniscient?
The answer my friend is when your life becomes irrelevant!

How many countries must a man travel,
before he's called well travelled?
The answer my friend, is on the horse he has saddled.
And how many poems must I write before you call me a poet?
The answer my friend, is that I already am, I just don't know it!
And how many sunsets do we have to
see, before we call it beautiful?
The answer my friend, is in the rainbow coloured waterfall!

How many women does a man have
to sleep with, to be satisfied?
The answer my friend, is that it doesn't matter, as he lied.
And how many wars must be lost, before
we realise there's no enemy?
The answer my friend, is in the evil of you and me!

And how many statues must we create, to worship false heroes?
The answer my friend, is we should never kiss their halos!
And how many times must we play
'Tambourine Man' till we call it a song?
The answer my friend, is that music can never be wrong!
And how many times can Bob Dylan be heard on our stereo?
The answer my friend, is when you stop tapping your toe.

And how many times must the quiet man make a suggestion?
The answer my friend, is when the answer becomes a question!
Yes *the answer my friend,* is a life long legacy,
The answer is all a part of our destiny!

The answer is 'blowing in the wind!'
The Answer is in everything we've binned

The Answer, is just an alternative Bob Dylan;
The answer is that man is 'ju*st like a woman!'*

Storm In A Teacup

The dark aroma, the stains
Of black coffee. Creating a storm
Cloud without milk…
The torrential rainstorm
As the boiling water gets added and the hailstones
Of sugar grains roar down!

The lightning strike
Of the teaspoon
And the crashing thunder
Of steel against china, the oozing
Of the teabag's flavour!

The steam that rises, like mist until the silver
Lining of the semi-skimmed milk
Eases the tension and anticipation…

The Rich Tea dips in like the sunset,
The storm in the teacup!

Windmills

Smoky bars, same old faces,
These eyes have seen so many places.
Same old stories on a Friday night
Walking home alone, under the pale moonlight
Nothing changes, all-round,
Reminding us, of that familiar sound…
Canned laughter and cheap thrills,
Constantly turning, like windmills.

Monday to Friday, nine to five,
Designer smiles to stay alive
Happy-go-lucky, this new generation,
Bashing out consumer masturbation!
Being single, married or just dating,
Tick, tock, tick, tock, the mind's calculating.
Fast food diet, microwave meals,
Expensive times, for cheap thrills,
You won't die young if you take these pills…
Same old story, going around, just like windmills.

Wishing On A G-string

I see the dust gathering around my guitar case
Instantly, I'm taken back to that special place.
I remember when my plectrum stroked your G-string.
I smile, a distant smile, just remembering.
It was in a smoky bar, off Tottenham Court Road
I was playing at the Borderline, when in you strode.
Leather trousers and black lace top
I remember thinking you were hot!
I was doing an acoustic version of
Madness's 'Driving In My Car!'
My eyes were fixed upon you at the bar!
You looked so lovely
Drinking your double straight JD,
You seemed to have not a care…
As you played with your hair
I played that U2 song
'Still Haven't Found What I'm Looking For!'
Whilst you danced in front of me, on the dance floor
Looking at me as you danced…
I was spellbound and in a trance!
And as I stroked my guitar's G-string
I was lost in a world of fantasising
And in that split second, when the audience clapped
My poor G-string suddenly snapped!
Flying out into the audience and to your feet
And as you bent down, I took a peep,
And saw your G-string, it was navy blue.
That was the night I met you.

Talking To A Tombstone

Cold hairs stick up on my neck
Sun's in the clouds, a little speck.
Morning dew, dampens the grass…
Reminding me, another year's past.
I've not forgotten. For every time the birds sing-
It reminds me, of everything…
Another year's past, and I have grown
As I find myself, talking, to a tombstone,
I look at the moss that's gathered around the edge,
I look to the side and see wild berries in the hedge.

I tell you about my day
I ask why you went away?
I smile, but I feel so much sadness,
I tell you you're truly missed.
I put the flowers by last year's bunch,
And tell you the news over lunch.
Time goes fast and I must get home
I feel better, talking to a tombstone.

I clean the grave with the hankie in my pocket,
I can hear you giggle telling me to stop it!
I tell you that I still love you
I still love you…
I never lied about that,
That's an eternal fact
I get up from wet knees…
The tears get colder in the breeze
I feel you by me, I'm not alone,
says me, talking to your tombstone.

Watching The Leaves Turn Green

Watching the leaves turn green,
Reminds me of the wonders I've seen,
The once bare branches, now shine with fauna,
Raising me out of my social trauma.
The simple things in life, give us hope,
More faithful than the Pope!

Watching the leaves turn green,
Reminds me of what has been,
Another season gone and a new one on its way.
Within silent moments when we can't say
Simple things to make one another smile,
Sometimes it's worth going that extra mile.
Watching the leaves turn green,
Reminds us it's not a dream,
The grey clouds pass and we see the sun again,
Bringing a little bit of happiness to all men,
Soothing pride and tarnished egos,
Realising that we're only human, not superheroes.

A Piss-Up, A Bird
And A Fight

I knew I was going
To have a fight!
There was something about that
November night,
I had a few cans at mine,
A couple of shots and a line
of Charlie. It's only a short bus ride
into town…We're meeting the boys
in the Rose and Crown.

James was there, already drunk;
And Colin was stoned
On super skunk!
"Where's Mark?" James says aloud;
"Forget him! Who's getting the next round?"
It's busy down the boozer
This evening. There are some boys
At the bar! They're well steaming!

One's acting the tough guy,
Like Charlie Sheen;
The little prick can only
Be sixteen. I leave it
For now - but I've got my eyes
On him. James has got me
A bitter. "Cheers Jim!"
Colin's talking to Lenny
Who's by his side. Some bird flashes
Me a smile; I take it in my stride.

I'll wait till she's drunk, then
I'll get a snog. I'll tell the lads I'm
Going to the bog. Whilst I'm doing a slash,
That kid comes in and starts
Smoking some hash. He makes some
Sort of joke…Makes light of
The subject whilst having
A smoke.

'What a prat!' I think,
Taking a mental note, boy…
I'd love to cut his throat! I follow
Him out, he doesn't hold
The door open. He is cruising to
Get his legs broken.
A few pints later, I notice
The little turd, chatting up
Some bird…

I pull my eyes away from
The football on the television, I grit
My teeth, I stare at
These fools in sweet recognition.
"Oi! Boys!" I call "Where's Lenny?"
"He's in the bog, spending a penny!
"Why mate, what's the matter?"
"Well ain't…
That Lenny's bird giving
That ponce the chatter?"

Lenny returns, he ain't
That mad, he says she was
Just a slag, I still think this guy's taking the
Piss! Then I see them kiss...
I watch him go to the bog
Again to do a piss, I follow him in
The boys say
Leave it...But I'm having this little git!

I walk in, he nods his
Head towards me, I come from
Behind and smash his head into
The lavatory. He falls bleeding
I pick him up by his balls. He screams!
I knock him flying
Into the condom machines!
I laugh in his face as he
Starts to cry, my fist
Wipes away the
Tears from his eye,

I sit back down with
The boys and get called
A prat. We agree we should
Leave, after that. Walking home
Colin's got a kebab
In his gob, Lenny calls him
A fat dirty slob...James is
Laughing, he finds that funny;
James taunts Colin, saying
He looks like a Teletubby!

Some birds from the pub
are on the other side of the road; James
Invites them back to his abode.
He reckons we'll get a shag and starts
Giving it the blag
As it turns out.
He was right!
Not bad really
For a Friday night;
A piss-up
A bird
And a fight!

The Smile Of Charlie

It had been a year since I'd seen Charlie
I didn't think he'd recognise me?
Charlie can't speak and has cerebral palsy;
Despite his groans, he can't communicate verbally.
But his face lit up when he saw me;
I realised then why I do this work so easily,
Because money can't pay to see the smile of Charlie!

Lost in his world that I can't understand;
When he wants his food, he'll raise his hand.
He chews on a cloth that helps him relax,
He knows its midday, because he gets snacks.
He gets upset when he can't go to the lavatory
But it's all worth it, to see the smile of Charlie!

Today, I took him to see if he was suitable elsewhere
Not from his home, but another day-care.
To see if another place he might like?
He got upset and his hand he did bite!
I agreed with Charlie that it wasn't all that!
His normal day-centre was better in fact;
When we got back to his old place, he looked at me;
And gave me a smile, the smile of Charlie!

Observational Bus Ride

I travel past the boarded up shops,
With the kids outside with their lollypops.
Why don't I ever get a lick from anyone?

I look up at the adverts
I can't believe the experts!
When I can't even trust myself!

I look at the litter in the curb…
I see the kids smoking herb.
Reminding when I was high!

I see the sexy woman in the mini skirt
I see how she loves to flirt…
But not to me on this bus!

I hear my mobile ring…
People pretend they don't hear a thing.
Could be an old girlfriend?

I see many faces taking fast paces outside,
As they take their day in their stride.
As I take, my observational bus ride.

London In The Rain

I love London in the rain!
The overcast skies reflect my pain
As I walk down the Embankment…
I feel the city's excitement.
I am a tourist in my own city
Washing away my pity.

I love London in the rain!
Not one day is ever the same
Shadows of the Gothic architecture…
Paint a very different picture.
Reminding me of my own meanings…
A Londoner who has feelings.

I love London in the rain!
Playing along, with it's game
Every corner has something new.
The grey skies show a glimpse of blue
A smile comes across my face
London in the rain, I love this place!

All In A Text

I don't think this is working out, I'm just not into you.
I'm attracted to the idea of us being together,
But it's not going to be a relationship.
I'm leading you down a false path of hope,
I don't think I can tell you face to face…
So I text you

'I love you…'

Drunk, walking home from a Friday night,
I wonder why I'm single?
And get my mobile phone out,
Scrolling down the names on my phone,
I see names that mean nothing to me,
One night stands, women from work, friends,
Names of women I wish I knew.
I miss you, I still want you,
I wonder how your life is?
So I text you

'Hi, how are you doing?'

The huge rollercoaster of life
Has made us lose contact.
My best friend and other mates
I always promise to call,
But never do. Still thinking about
The good old days. All those fun
Times we had…I never said
Thanks for being a friend.
So I text,

'Hi mate, long-time-no-hear!'

I look at this little master of technology,
When I was a teenager, we never had this!
It was writing letters, or phone calls…
Words, feelings, were expressed
From a stuttering mouth
So I pick up the phone, say *'hello'*
On your answer phone.
You reply back

In a text.

I Wrote The B-Sides

I don't expect you to know
Where I came from.
This doesn't mean
You know I'm wrong.
These scribbling, powerful lyrics I write…
The feelings that kept me awake at night.
I listen to the latest number one
On the radio and I know…

I wrote the B-sides!

Looking into the eyes of
Those who live alone. Two young lovers
Walk by hand in hand, their gaze
Briefly catches mine but they
Don't understand. The song she
Hums happily to herself…
That I…

Wrote the B-sides!

I sit in the corner of the local pub,
Tucked away, I see everyone come
In every day…the drunks, the hard-nuts
The men and women on the pull
Yes in my corner, I see it all…
The girl goes to the jukebox
To put on her favourite song.
I see the boy claiming he's
Done nothing wrong, they kiss
And make up, but as it plays
In the background;
She'll never know That….

I wrote the B-sides!

I go about my way; a drifter
In my city
And I think it is a pity...that people
Make money from my thoughts,
And I admit it takes all sorts,
For them to recognise, that I...

Wrote the B-sides.

No Wires In The Sand

The hot, soft crystal-like texture of the sand,
Melts my feet, as I relax, beer in hand.
Sun warms my bare skin,
As the waves splash against my shin.
The sea breeze smells slightly salty,
And for once in my life I have tranquillity.
The Sun casts shadows on the rock face,
This beats, logging onto Myspace!
One thing I know that's true,
Is this is better than chatting on Yahoo.
Nature is real, the Internet's a fraud!
Time consuming, lifeless, it makes me bored.
But on this beach, I understand
Life's better with no wires in the sand.

21st Century; Little Red Riding Hood

It was on the edge of the city, in a downtown neighbourhood,
Where we encounter, our 21st Century little Red Riding Hood.
She was of an age of sexual maturity,
If I had to guess, I would say about twenty?
She did not actually own many clothes of red,
But she did go to her Grandma one day, when she was ill in bed.
Her father, worked as a self-employed car mechanic,
He suffered from depression, I think it was manic?

Her Dad became ill, when their Mother died,
Found hanging from a tree one day, suicide.
She had a sister, but she lived in another land,
And a brother, but he was touring with his band.
Little Red Riding Hood, was actually called Claire,
She was a petite, beautiful woman, with long red hair.
The call came through one morning, about Granny being ill,
Little Red Riding Hood had to go and
visit her and use her skill.
Dressed in her leather coat and her little red beanie hat,
She went off to her Granny, who lived in a flat.

The skies suddenly turned from blue to grey,
And so for shelter she choose a different way,
The rain came pouring down, as she knew it would,
So she took a longer, but drier way through the wood.
She had done this trip many times.
She loved the smell of flowers and pines.
But today she felt like she was being watched from the trees,
Felt the hairs on the back of her neck begin to freeze.
The woods became ghostly quiet,and sinister,
Dark thoughts came into her head
about her Mum and her sister.

The flickering of light from within the clearing,
Was her Grandmother's house, but from
afar she heard screaming!
She ran into the house and saw the place totally trashed,
All her stuff on the floor, drawers open and furniture smashed.
She ran upstairs and saw her Grandmother in bed,
She screamed when she saw the stains of crimson red.
Her Grandmother's throat had been slashed
and had bruises on her face,
Whoever did this was still in the place!
As if her thoughts exposed the truth,
She heard a voice behind her, cold and aloof.
"Well, well, well! What do we have here?"
She just froze in fear...

When she looked round, she saw a man in jeans and a t-shirt,
He had blood on his hands, but he didn't seem hurt?
"What big eyes you have!" he told her,
"And what beautiful breasts you have and beautiful hair,
You have eyes that can see beauty,
But sadly for you, they also see me!
You look as good as your friend here did,
I strongly advise not to try and hide like she did!"
He laughed then, a laugh of pure evil;
"ha, ha, she hid in her bed
And now look at her all cosy and dead!"

Little Red Riding Hood, near to the
stairs, she had a chance to run,
She screamed; " That was my Grandmother, you scum!"
He licked the blood from his fingers and laughed;
His eyes beckoned to the stairs; "you want a head start?"
Little Red Riding Hood made a run for it,
Ran for her life, from this lunatic,
Out the door and into the woods, she went to hide;
She was shaking, she was petrified!
The cold voice of the stranger was close as well,
"Hmm!" he shouted; "you have a fragrant smell,
When I find you, which I will for sure,
I am going to rape you, then bury you under this forest floor"

Claire ran deeper and deeper into the wood;
She heard the voice say;
"Now, now, come here my little Red Riding Hood"
To her delight she saw the edge of town and she ran to safety,
Only to fall over a branch and smash her knee!
The sudden force that hit her back, echoed the laugh;
As rough bloodied hands went round her neck, with a scarf!
And as she gasped and fought to breathe…
She felt his hand go up her dress, the dirty sleaze;
And as she felt his hands pull her hair
From a distance, she heard a voice, from somewhere.

"Help" it was spoken, more than a scream;
But it must have worked, as the voice was now seen;
She saw her rescuer's face. It was bleak and sad.
But she smiled at this face, as it was her Dad.
Shouting began, and a fight occurred,
Fists were thrown and insults were slurred
The Grandmother's attacker lay still on the forest path,
No more could she hear that laugh
Her Dad picked her up and into his arms,
Away from the wood and all its harms,
That night, father and daughter, after talking to the police;
Found solace in pain and love, through grief.
Claire told her Dad what happened in all its glory;
About the real little Red Riding Hood story!

The Devil's Desire

In the sprawling clouds of the electrical storm,
The cracks on the citadel walls do form
They mirror the cracks upon a beating heart,
The silence of laughter is far apart.

The mirrors cast shadows of the Devil himself!
Next to the dusty books upon the shelf,
Lay huge hands, with tight black veins
Holding his head that hides his pains!

Two, long grey horns protrude from his head!
Eyes sunken, like the living dead!
The thunder rages with so much power,
The lightning strikes the black-bricked tower!

Just like his heart of stone,
A green fungus grows around his throne.
As he weeps and screams like a hurricane,
His blood is scalded by his pain.

Turning his head, he looks out the window pane,
Watching how mortals play their game..
Outside the window;
He sees emotions on the Earth below,
His sadness shows he'll never know…

What it is to love!

Change

I used to think Change was strange,
It made me shiver and go deranged!
'What if?' and 'what will?'
How and what will I feel?

Safe and comfortable in my zone,
Knowing the boundaries, around my home,
Like a pawn in a game of chess
Heading into certain death.

Shrewd and clever, never losing face
As the Queen now stands in its place,
I feel like the lucky pawn
Embracing a new dawn.

Knowing that change can be beneficial,
And that change is essential!
I know that emotions are a phase.
No escape until someone pays!

Feelings are mixed with excitement,
A feeling of achievement.
I'm that pawn heading towards salvation
About to embrace the celebration.

Triumphant, victorious, changing the game!
It's boring if things stay the same.
Change is here, change is good
although at times, misunderstood.

Lancelot's Wound

The story of Lancelot's wound, is a legendary tale!
About love, friendship and betrayal!
Lust mixed with love, of a woman that was not his.
But nothing mattered, when they kissed.
Arthur, was not only his King, but also his friend
In which he would search for the Grail, to the bitter end!
England was dying and so was the King,
There seemed no arrival, to the season of spring.
Barren were the lands, pestilent and plagued!
The Queen stood by her King, but she was easily swayed.
Guinevere was as beautiful as her Celtic charm,
She never meant to hurt the King and bring him harm!
As Arthur, sunk into depression, Lancelot looked on,
Within the arms of the Queen; he knew he'd done wrong!
He fled into the forest and sought shelter, from his shame!
But this was only the beginning of Lancelot's pain.
That evening Guinevere came to him and they made love under
the sky,
But in their passion Lancelot rolled on to his sword, and let out
a cry!
"What have I done? I have betrayed my King! My Friend! And
My Country!"
Guinevere tried to comfort him, but he
screamed "Don't look at me!"
Lancelot went into exile and became a man with no name,
Riddled with guilt of his actions and sickened by shame!
Guinevere spent her days in a convent, drenched in her sins!

Years went by and Arthur became stronger, his mind on other things,
England was at war, fighting the betrayal of his sister and son,
His sister Morgana, who believed England was hers and was there to be won!
But when all seemed doomed and Arthur would never see another day,
A figure approached the traitor, Morgana Le Faye.
The great mace swung with such power and force,
Full of anger, hatred and bitter remorse!
Morgana slumped to the ground, dead!
Lancelot picked up his lance and rammed it into Mordred's head!
His eyes then glanced over to his King in battle, needing assistance
And with a battle frenzy, Lancelot came to his king with no hesitance.
Bodies of the enemy were flung to their death,
Lancelot then got struck on his side, which took his breath.
He managed to get to his King, his friend, and joined him in union,
As they lay dying, it was an emotional fusion
Arthur looked into his friends eyes, and smiled, "You came back for me.."
Lancelot just cried, "My King, I beg you to forgive me"
Blood was gushing from Lancelot's side, as by Arthur he kneeled,
And whispered "My lord it is the old wound, it never healed"
Now the final words from Arthur may or may not be true?
As he held Lancelot's head in his arms, he whispered, "I forgive you....."

History

In battles, in conflict and in wars,
Peace isn't bought in superstores!
Sucked right in like dirty whores,
Hearts washed up upon the shores.
Blamed on one's insanity,
What we learnt from our history?

Tales told by a jealous tongue,
Putting down someone.
Whispers fly after the setting sun,
Blamed for a crime they've not done,
Now labelled a evil scum.
Has it benefited us being so nasty?
What we learnt from our history?

Religions are used, to explain the unknown,
To bring hope to those alone,
Ruled by a man on a throne,
Dictated to those at home!
Have we profited from Christianity?
What we learnt from our history?

Reason and thought, blessed are we,
Which we've used for hypocrisy,
We think 'It doesn't bother me,'
But when it does who looks silly?
Yet, it's wiped away so quickly.
What we learnt from our history?

We've lost so much time being angry!
Hell-bent on ruining a lovely memory.
We think we know, what we don't see,
And go about our days, so foolishly.
In a brave bid to be happy,
What we learnt from our history?

Poems That You'll Never See

There are poems that you'll never see,
Marked in a folder titled 'privacy!'
Poems of hate and anger and personal pain,
Poems oncecrning greed, hunger and personal gain!
Poems about people I would love to see dead!
Poems about women I want in my bed.
Poems regarding relationships that have gone bad,
Poems on issues with Mum and Dad.
Poems about me, the person no one knows.
Poems about places where my soul only goes.
Poems I could place in the clouds, for all to read!
Poems about lust, selfishness and greed.
Poems I know will hurt those I hate!
Poems I've written by mistake.
Poems I have hidden in my heart and my head,
Poems about things that are better left unsaid.
Poems I want to share and poems I want to retract!
Poems of shame and how others may act.
They stay in my psyche, they're part of me,
These poems I write, but you'll never see!

Jester of Shadows

I am the Jester of Shadows!
Smiles and jokes fall on deaf ears
In the gloomy courtroom.
I talk about death, in front of thousands,
I recite tales of doom.
As the Lords and Kings,
Wallow in their own grief!
I dance, like a silhouette.

In my costume of grey and black,
Fingers so slight, I play my lute.
I spellbind my audience,
Into a soulless coma.
But it is not me that lives in despair!
Not me who doesn't smile or laugh!
Not me that lives under
A constant rain cloud.

I don't only have stories of doom,
I too have grieved,
But I have moved on!
I dance in the moonlight
My skin is not grey or black,
But pure white!
My fingers have caressed
Pure beauty!

Darkness is an easy audience,
For it is a job, like all others,
Because I dance for the depressed,
Does not make me depressed!
Because I work in darkness,
Does not mean I live there!
Maybe I'll appear at your shows?
I am the Jester of Shadows!

The Butterfly Collector

I look out upon my creation,
In my backyard, the Garden of Eden!
A mixture of beauty and sin.
I hold in my palm, something
So beautiful, it even makes God cry!

This unique and adorable butterfly,
So small, so lovely, so special to me.
I painted her wings, blue like the sea,
I made her eyes black, like a shadowy evening.
And with my kiss, I started her breathing.

Her white body was like the virgin snow,
As I held her, I never wanted to let go.
I'm God, powerful, and all-knowing,
From my words, I made the sun glowing,
But look at me now, lost for words and thought.
From this little creature, so much she's taught
Me about freedom and change and pure beauty.
This butterfly meant so much to me!
I couldn't keep this divine creature for myself,
The world would die without her wealth!

She would breathe life into the flowers,
Her tears would make them grow like rain showers,
She would be the sunset and the moonrise!
She'd place the stars within the skies!
She'd make mankind feel warm inside,
She'll be the crushing waves of the tide,
How could I keep this wonderful butterfly?
So I created my soul, as the dragonfly!

The Animal Within

It was only a scratch, it just broke the skin,
Never did I dream of what it would bring!
A walk through the woods, a short cut home.
Yes, I know I should never walk through the woods alone.
But my path was well lit, by the full moonlight,
And I had done this walk, many a night.
I never saw the creature that flashed past me,
This creature which would set this monster free!

I saw the lights of my home, burning bright…
My family's silhouettes, inside, safe and alright!
The smell of saliva and scent of human flesh,
The scratch across my face, a shadow across my breath!
I touched my cheek and I looked at my bloodied hand,
Till this day, even now, I don't fully understand
Shaken, I felt adrenaline pump around my veins,
I ran to my home with a fever in flames!

My wife attended to me with a frantic pace,
She said I had claw marks upon my face.
I looked out through my misty window,
And looked at my reflection, a distorted fellow.
I see the woods, the trees, the feeling of fear,
So far away, but yet so near.
The following days, my body never felt so good,
My fat stomach became as hard as wood!

My muscles tightened, and my senses became clearer,
And I felt the fear come nearer and nearer!
I looked at my daughter, who is only three,
And started thinking, she's not like me?
The sex between me and my wife became rough!
She would scream "Stop! Enough!"
I would bite her, scratch her and pull her hair!
She said I had an animal's look, a wolf's stare.

Weeks went by and I became one with nature,
I had a bizarre bond with an unseen creature,
A human or a wolf, a monster that haunted me!
In my dreams and in my nightmares, for me to see,
It was about a month later that I felt my scar burn,
I felt this creature inside of me start to turn.

Upstairs in the bedroom, I stepped through the door,
Where the full moon's shadow was cast on the floor!
My screams turned to howls!
I fell to my knees!
My insides fell through my bowels
Hair came through my skin at an alarming rate!
As my skull merged into a monster, I knew my fate!
My arms became legs and my hands, claws
My feet had vanished and were now paws!

Teeth became fangs, my clothes now torn!
The creature of hate was now reborn!
Blood, screams, death, guilt, fear and hate
But when I awoke, it was all too late!
My wife! Well what was left of her,
Her mutilated body, blood mixed with fur,
Then my daughter, whose stomach had been eaten
And her severed head, broken and beaten!

I walked out of the door and into the wood…
A man, an animal, something misunderstood!
As the sun shone, from the bright blue sky,
I went into the forest, to die!
I touched my face, only a scratch, just broke the skin,
But just enough to awaken, the animal within!

Defending The Faith

I look back at my rain-trodden footprints,
From my mud-stained, leather boots.
I hear the clattering of my sword
Against my chain mail,
The sword, stained with blood
A sword that has served an infrastructure,
Which I am paid to uphold.

I do not fight for my faith,
But for the gold coins,
I feel the weight of my purse,
Like the guilt on my shoulders!

The steam from my breath,
Is a vapour so foul!
Like my soul, dark,
Twisted and broken!
And they say…
He made us in his own image

My God, who I kill for,
Must be a mercenary?

I look at the 'red cross' tunic I wear,
And learn to hate that
which I have become!
Slain children and women,
old and young,
Looked death in the eyes,
And past others over to him..God forgives
Murder in battle, I was told.

And as I return back
To the village from once all this started
I see the priest on his golden throne!
The serfs plough their rotting lands!
I see my reflection in the muddy puddle.
A false hero stares back at me!
Cheering breaks my thoughts,
I've come back a hero,
For defending the faith!

Fallen Angel

Like silver eyes, staring out from a vacuum of darkness,
The stars of Heaven this evening glow with sadness.
The shooting star looks not quite right tonight?
Its trailing flames look out of sight.

I see her wings, dirty and scorched!
Like an unwanted toy, abused and debauched.
For this is no star, that falls from Heaven's home,
This is a fallen Angel, now all alone!

I heard her scream, as she fell,
But I guide her gently, away from Hell.
"Fallen Angel, you are not forgotten!
For what is Heaven, but elitist and rotten!"

"Fall sweet Angel, into the palm of my hands,
For here, you will be safe, within my lands.
Cast off your wings, and please don't cry,
I will breathe life into, you will not die!"

This Angel fallen, from outer space,
Looks upon me with a smile on her face
Her gaze as mysterious as the evening sky,
She looks at me, and asks; "Why?"

My hands gently brush against her wings,
"Why?" I say, "Why do you think the bird sings?"
She shakes her head, not knowing what I mean,
I tell her, "They sing to wake us from our dream!"

"But here you are, safe within these worlds I bear
You will never fall again, my Angel, I swear!"
Her wings, like her halo, begin to shine
I tell her that she's free to leave, as she is not mine!

"For angels are for all to share"
I tell her, as I fix her wings with gentle care.
Now my Angel, you have a choice,
As I look up to Heaven and raise my voice!

"God of fools, hear me speak!
You have cast down your Angel. alone and weak!
But my power is strong and I have brought her back,
She comes in peace, not to attack!"

Dawn breaks and the birds sing so gay,
"My Angel, you have a choice, go back, or stay
Her star-like eyes, looked deep into me,
"It's your world that I wish to see."
As she makes her choice, the sun shines anew,
As the night sky turns a shade of blue,
The wind is warmer now, as she fades from sight,
My fallen Angel, graceful in flight.

Listening to Mark

You've been taken for a mug!
What can you do,
But laugh and shrug?
Only a bird mate, after all...
Just move on, it's all cool
Go out have a beer, maybe a few?
And get back to the life you once knew!
Laugh, smile and meet new girls.
How about that barmaid with the pigtails?
She'll do, no baggage, just a fun loving bird,
Don't get caught up
In the game mate, that's absurd.
When it's over, it's over,
Don't beat yourself up about it,
After all, a tit's a tit.
I know she got right down
Low and in your head,
But look on the bright side,
She was good in bed!
Lessons mate, that's
What it's all about,
Forget about that old trout!
Plenty more fish in the sea,
You'll be ok, you'll
Soon see. New job, new paths
To take. How about that girl
Last night, for heaven's sake!

You think too much and
you're still grieving your Mum,
So don't beat yourself up, she
Just weren't the One. Just call it
An adventure or something,
Just keep on doing what you're doing…
You're a good bloke, one of a kind…
You just need to
Get her out of your mind.
And stop going on and on about the spark!
When you going to listen, to your mate Mark?

Matt The Drummer Boy

I am Matt the Drummer Boy, whose broken
Drumsticks mirror my heart.
Upon this oak tree I lay, injured and dying...
Overlooking the aftermath of such
A bloody battle.!
All of them dead!
All of them who have died to my drumbeat.
Women I once loved, once drummed for...
Beating to the rhythm of my heart,
All our dead, all have gone
No-one remains.
I tap on my drum, looking at all the heartache
I have wasted, but no more battles
For me...Or at least that's what I
Thought laying here...But the humming
Near me is no bee.
For no bird that I know sings this song,
No flower that I know smells so sweet.
And as I close my eyes,
I hear the wind sing to me;
"Play just one last time for me, Matt
My little drummer boy."
With my eyes closed, and close to
Death, I whisper;
"I have no love left to give
No passion to play my drum,
Oh sweet and beautiful wind."
I feel the wind become warmer,
Like that of summer
"My little drummer boy, it was
I that saved you from the battle!"

Anger rages within me
"A battle I never wanted!"
"But a battle that we all must face
My little drummer boy!"
"How can I trust you?
How I can continue with my heart so bloody?"
"Because now, my drummer boy
You have been rewarded."
My eyes open, I feel
Death takes a back seat
Curiosity may well be my saviour?
"How?" I say, as I feel
My fingers play the drum gently.
The wind around me blew hard
And blossom fell from the tree.
And as my eyes, slowly opened,
I played...my drum!

A Letter To Galway

I sit here now,

Listening to Nick Cave's new CD, remembering when we
went to see him at Brixton Academy. Arms round your waist,
holding you tight. That still goes down as my most wonderful
night. I don't know what made me so mad? I shared with you
my life; told you about Dad. Never really done that before, let
someone be so close, your lips were like the sweetest red rose.

As the Pulp song goes, "We were friends, that's as far
as it went." Although I pursued you with a lust-fuelled
intent! I lost a friend, because of my madness
A battle which killed kindness. Going to those gigs, hand in
hand, in love with you, but nothing was planned. Late night
drinking in the Spinning Wheel, me not knowing what to feel!

My heart cut open when you went away.
My mouth dried up with no words to say.
When you told me you were going to Australia; God, how
I missed ya. I wrote those stupid emails, ranting and raving
about drunken Irish girls! I remember walking on China's
Great Wall, thinking what an idiot I was, a complete fool!

Then I put your photo on "Hot or Not" Just to see what
score you got. And that was my worst and final mistake
and the last contact I would ever make. So many years
ago now, since we last said hello, but I am writing you this
letter, just to let you know. That although this poem you
will never read, this is one wound that will always bleed!
I still think about you now, till this very day. So I am
writing you this letter, to the West coast of Galway.

The Return of the Prince

Walking into the edge of town
Wearing my 'strangers frown'
You thought I would never come back!
But I have, I am still dressed in my armour, of mythical black!
My swords are now sharper than ever
And the smell of blood is still mixed with heather…
I have been away, but now I have come to take what's mine!
I find an Inn and have some stale bread and wine.

I am still that dark stranger in the corner in the shadows,
As mysterious and as dark as the gallows!
I am still a Prince, I am still a knight and I am still a guru.
I have been away in exile, thinking of you!
And I have come back to the place where I was once banished,
Although I have dents in my armour, I am not damaged.
I pay for a room in the Inn for a few nights,
I whisper to the innkeeper amongst the fights.

He agrees to feed me and attend to my steed,
I like this man; he gives for friendship, not greed,
He does not know it, but he has made an important friend.
I go upstairs and prepare for tomorrow's end.
I attend to my swords and shields,
Looking out the window, towards the green, muddy fields.
I fall into a slumber, so deep and needed,
It has been many moons since I have feuded.

The next day, I head to the middle of the village,
Amidst the chaos of the town's frantic spillage,
They don't notice another stranger in a black cloak,
Although my accent gave me away last time I spoke.
Large swords and battle-axes are not new here,
The town is buzzing with excitement and fear,
I slip in and out of the angry mob's cries,
My hand grips my sword. Today, everyone dies!

From the gap under my cloak, I see what I've come for,
A woman tied to a stake, naked,
With a scar across her chest saying, *whore!*
I barge myself past these foolish villagers,
Whose minds are like evil scavengers!
I stand in front of the woman;
She is pale, tears run down her face,
I get myself into position and find myself some space.
Over to the far side of the crowd, the innkeeper I see,
He raises his hands, he has brought my horse for me.
The priest of the town goes to set fire
to the wood around the girl,
I know now, if I lose this battle, all will fail!

I throw back my cloak and show myself to the crowd,
Everyone stops, the gasps of those fools is so loud!
For the Dark Prince has returned, to
save his woman from death!
And to kiss her once more and give her life from his breath
I slice arms, heads, legs, women and men!.
Death would come, but they didn't know when!

I cut the ropes that bound my vampire,
I put her over my shoulder and escaped the burning fire!
The innkeeper does his part and passes me my horse,
We jump on and leave the dying behind. I have no remorse!
Still men try and grab her, trying to pull her off me,
I slay these fools, none will stand in the way of our destiny!
The smell of blood stirs my vampire back to life...
"I told you I would not leave you, my wife!"

Online Romance

Emotions, through a keyboard, through wires,
Phone calls, web cams,
Madness beyond madness.
For reality is where true love lives
Not at my desk, with no boundaries.
Yet ever since I got this computer,
I have lusted and loved,
More times in my whole life,
Yet in reality, I have been hidden,
Tucked away, put into a file,
Like a high school project…Yet
Confusion, hurt, pain, warmth, love and lust!
All seem to come from the same place.
And even in cyberspace,
Hearts can be broken. Friends can be made,
And lovers met.
I am a good man, a unique individual.
I deserve something…
I am wasted being alone.
Yet in the real world, I am not alone,
I have friends, family and a social life,
So why I am drawn to this Internet?
Why does love and lust hunt me down?
Why do I allow myself to get hurt?
Make friends, lose friends, make friends!
It's a circle I have been trapped in,
Yet I am thinking now I will break it…
Reality is better than reading emails,
To kiss the lips of life is better than kissing a screen!
Maybe now I will cut my losses,
Maybe go into exile?
Exile being reality!

Falling In Love
Star Wars Style

Falling in love my way,
Well, what is there to say?
Try imagining that scene in the Empire Strikes Back,
When Luke faces Darth Vader, that villain in black!
Vader tells Luke he is his father and asks to join him,
And Luke loses his hand and jumps into that pit thing!
When someone says they love me,
I warp into another galaxy?

Luke lost his hand, but I have lost my heart!
I'm falling head over heels, I'm falling apart.
My light sabre is still my great phallic weapon,
Constantly waiting for something to happen,
Not yet a Jedi, as yet the dark side still lurks inside,
Unable to choose between the good and the bad side,
Those dirty thoughts in my head, our the dark side of the force!
Like intergalactic intercourse!

I will defeat the evil Sith Lord!
I will break away from my umbilical cord!
I will rule the universe,
No matter how perverse.
I will become a real Jedi Knight!
Falling in love, my biggest fight,
Dark side or good side I must choose,
Falling in love with you, means I never lose.

Earth Angel

She touches me softly, upon my heart of glass,
She makes me feel and my heart pumps fast,
Every thought is a feeling, so loving and warm,
An emotion so new, it has never been born,
A truth that burns, which only lovers know,
I long for that kiss, so loving, so slow,
You are my Earth Angel, sent down for me,
You touch my soul, across the sea
I wait for your tenderness, but I never know when,
But when my dreams become reality, I know it is then.

Katie

From the branches of the trees that expand in this busy city,
I peer down and look at you, Katie.
I don't suppose you'll remember me?
Especially in this form, a bird in a tree,
But I've never left you, Katie.

I don't know how long it's been in human years?
I still hear you call me at night, in your tears.
I feel your love, high above in the sky
That sparrow in your garden, is I!
I fly above our old house and at dawn, I sing to you,

I perch on your window,
But you have no clue.
I never left you Katie…
I've been reincarnated you see.

You'll always be a part of me!
I fly with you above the city,
My heart carries you inside of me…
I never left you, Katie!

The Sycamore Tree

Many dawns he had seen,
Leaves had turned from brown to green,
Then from green to brown,
Every time the sun went down.

Tall and proud, it stood within the meadow,
Sheltering many a stranger from rain and snow.
Even the weeds respected him!
He looked so beautiful in the spring.

It was upon one of these days,
When Mother Nature gifted him one of her strays…
A woodpecker came and sat on his branch to rest,
He was not bothered, as many birds had laid their nest.

He then heard, then felt the peck,
Like a love bite on his neck.
His hard bark began to crumble on the ground below,
He tried to shout for the bird to go.

But the bird seemed not to be evil or bad,
Rather it was lonely, needy and sad.
And as the moon came up and the sun went down,
In the distance came the sound of town.

The woodpecker created her home, within the tree,
And nestled into his heart so comfortably.
The tree's tough bark had never been damaged,
Let alone broken and ravaged!

He liked the feeling of having someone inside,
He felt his roots strengthen with pride.
Then one day, the woodpecker flew away,
And did not return at the end of the day!

Days turned to weeks, weeks to years!
The sap of the tree cried his tears.
And the tree stood alone again,
With a hole in its trunk, empty with pain!

For he loved the woodpecker,
Although he never said.
And she loved him,
As she lay in the next field,
Dead!

The Rock And The Sheep

The little sheep that grazed upon the rich green grass,
Didn't always have a joyful past.
Her woolly coat which glistened like pure snow,
Was once muddy and tattered not long ago.
I was the rock in the field,
I saw her past, present and what the future would yield!
I had always admired her, but I had never been heard,
I felt powerless, as I saw the abuse she incurred.

She sang to the other sheep, with poetry in her baa's,
They did not see that beneath her wool were atrocious scars!
I saw what the shepherds did to her!
I saw the way the farmer ripped off her fur!
As she stood upon her hills of green and grey,
Knowing that tomorrow was another day.
I called out to her, "Be strong! Believe
in yourself, just I like I do!"
But she never heard me. Rocks can't
speak, in case you never knew.

She refused to eat the grass and she became weak,
Whilst I mastered a way to speak
She used to cut herself on the barbed wire fence,
Reliving the pain she felt inside, the cutting became intense!
Then one day, I don't know how? Something changed?
Through her madness, she had become deranged!
She came up to me one day…
And said; "you're the rock that has been
with me and never turned away!"
I said, "No, I never turned away my little sheep, that's true,
I have seen what they have done to you!"
She bowed her head and nuzzled herself to me
"Will you? My rock, will you keep me company?"
"Always, my sheep, always…!"
And I kept that promise, till the end of her days.

Blockbuster Babe

Whilst I look at the latest DVD,
I think I see her notice me?

I feel myself go to pieces,
When she stocks the new releases

I can just about look up her skirt,
I see her long red hair, against her blue shirt.

In my confusion, I find myself looking at porn!
I then get all embarrassed and drop my popcorn.

In my head I am saying; "just ask her out Matt!"
But the shop is busy and I might look a prat?

I think she is from Eastern Europe or around that part?
I know right now, she is in my heart!

I think about us having sex on DVD's,
I should get an Oscar for my fantasies!

The girl in Blockbusters is my sexy dame;
But I don't leave with her number,
just another Playstation game!

Liking Too Many, Kissing Too Few

I am judging too many people here,
Yet it's really me, I judge I fear,
Standing at the bar, with a beer,
My eyes are glued to her rear,
Long legs and long hair,
But that's all I do, stare!
I don't know what to do?
When I'm liking too many and kissing too few.

What I Did For Love

These were the final thoughts before I died............

Vampires! Just stories right?
Made to scare us and give us a fright,
Oh, how I wish that was true,
I only did it because of you.
I did it because I wanted us to be together forever,
My human lust, my mortal endeavour.
From the moment I saw you
I loved you. I wanted you!
A photo on my computer screen,
I wanted more, than just a dream.
As my sun sets and your moon rises,
My soul gently wept, to new surprises.
Obsessed, crazed like a wolf in heat!
With my plan in hand, I took to the street.
I heard stories told by the sailors down by the docks.
Of women selling sex in 'knocking shops.'
But these women sold more than sex, they sold desires!
But even then, they were stories, stories of vampires!
The moon was full and the clouds were gone,
In my heart of hearts, I knew this was wrong.
Down winding alleyways and sunken paths,
I followed the screams, or were they laughs?
The smell of the sea air and the sound of laughter,
I soon came face to face with what I was after!
Her face glistened in the pale light of the moon!
I slipped her some money and she took me to a room.
Without a word, she pulled me close and on to the bed,
And soon I was making love to the undead!
She lay there inviting, her legs open wide,

She then bit my neck, and a part of me died,
The feeling was that of heroin, but so much stronger,
I felt powerful, fit, healthy and younger!
The lust, which I carried for you
Took on something completely new.
I took the whore in my embrace
And with a blood filled hunger, devoured her face!
The window was open and I so flew out,
Now my love, I will show you, what a vampire is all about.
Across the sea I flew with lightning pace,
With such guile and beauty and birdlike grace.
I knew where you lived, for I had your address,
I hovered outside your window, I watched you undress.
I cast a spell of knowing and lust
You let me in, for in me you did trust,

I was not the man you talked to online,
Tonight I was yours and you were mine.
As we lay naked, on top of your unmade covers,
We were what I wanted, two unbreakable lovers!
I bit your neck and you bit mine,
The pain was like our lovemaking, simply divine.
Embraced in our sins, the time went too soon,
I failed to notice the dropping moon
As the rays of dawn came through the window pane,
Touching our backs, we burst into flame!

Just Daydreaming

I sit on this rock that has been my life,
Shuddering as the sea breeze scorns my cheeks.
I look out into the pale blue horizon,
Gripping to my self-conscious,
Struggling to find a meaning,
Just me alone, daydreaming.

The savageness of what I have seen,
And the places that I've been.
Awaken something I thought was buried,
But even in death, I guess you can die?
In my heart, I hear the young child screaming,
Just me alone, daydreaming!

The pale yellow stains of the cliffs behind me,
And the rapturous orange and red sky,
Cast shadows over all my visions.
And as I close my eyes, I have this feeling,
That I'm not alone, just daydreaming.

Sandcastles In The Sky

From the reflections of my dreams,
You see my ideas, and hare-brained schemes,
I chuckle to what may have been.
My self-esteem becomes a natural high,
As I build sandcastles in the sky.

The little blue bucket and spade, I have by my side,
I bashfully bury my head in the sand to hide.
And even though my first attempts fail, I know I tried,
I learnt from my mistakes and now I know why...
As I build my sandcastles in the sky!

The sandcastles are a colour of red, not yellow,
Because my blood is stronger than any fellow!
Although, I have a quick temper, for a man so mellow.
At least I'm comfortable being a man who can cry,
As I build my sandcastles in the sky.

The blue sky above mirrors the sea,
And the seagulls circle around me.
The cool, fresh seaside air makes me see,
That if I put my mind to things and try,
As I build my sandcastles in the sky.

How Blue Became Green

Imagine if you will, a castle on a hill,
Overlooking rivers, meadows and towers,
A world, very similar to ours.
Within this castle are many kings,
Talking about important things.
An uneasy concern marks their faces,
As they clutch their swords, shields and maces!
At the head of this table,
Is a king without a label.

He announces to the other kings,
That when day breaks, the birds don't sing?
Their troubled faces only stare ,
They are worried that their fields are bare.
The king without the label carries on,
"My kings!" he says, "Our God is gone!"

The religion of this land,
Is something we may find hard to understand.
They worshiped a God called Blue.
And across the land, Blue was true!
The word of Blue was written in a book,
So everybody could have a look.

The meeting of the kings was about the demise of Blue
Without religion, what could they do?
The greatest king without a label,
Demanded calm around the table.
"Blue!" he said, "Is officially dead!"
The kings agreed, with nodding heads,
Without Blue, what would people say?
Maybe turn from Blue to Grey?

The new religion, they decided, will be called Green!
And they agreed, it would be the best religion ever seen!
But what would they tell the people in the towns?
The kings looked sullen, with knowing frowns.
They agreed to tell them that Blue was to blame,
And that Green will not be the same.
Spread the word that Blue brought evil to the land!
And soon everyone will understand.

Years went by and Green did spread
People turned their backs on Blue,
And worshiped Green instead!
Soon Green become so over-rated,
Until everybody became so frustrated!
People soon walked out of town,
To worship another religion....Brown!

Painting A Blazing Sunset

The blood that drips from my wrist
Scatters across the canvas sky,
Sunken black eyes,
Like two blackbirds, returning to spring.
Green fields of envy, burn so bright,
Which silhouettes the ground at night.

Fingers broken on dry skin,
Clouds absorb the suffering.
Tears that stream down my face,
Create a sea of stars in space.

Boiling point of emotions,
Paint a blazing sunset!
Scabs from old wounds,
Like mountain ranges of jagged peaks,
And hope.

The beginning of dawn
Gives rise to peace,
Spilling a rainbow of magical colours,
With no gold at the end,
Just me!

Stardust

Reaching up, hands burn through Earth's skies,
Blistering my skin and bringing water to my eyes.
Touching the star, grabbing it, holding it, and make it mine!
Squeezing it's soul to dust so fine,
Stardust, magic, so pure and true,
I sprinkle it's contents all over you.

Watch as dust sinks into your skin,
And wait, for the magic to begin.
Stardust, so rare the most valuable powder.
Stops all pain, getting louder;
Brings smiles and tears to your face,
And happiness and peace to the human race.

Stardust, I took from the sky above me,
It burns my arms and hands, plain to see.
But someone had to do it, bring magic back,
And cast our hearts out of black
Stardust, let me sprinkle some on you,
Making all your dreams come true.

Gentlemanly Virtue

Upon this journey I have created, which has no end.
I ride a steed of honesty, love and sensitivity.
I carry a sword that is only meant for evil,
The evil that men do and to avenge men's souls!
I carry a Bible that mentions no God,
Only poems and tales of truth and despair!
Upon my journey, I have read your poems,
I know the issues and pain that you have faced.
But I am a warrior of gentlemanly virtue,
And will not turn around now to head back,
For I have been infected upon this journey,
With a parasite, so deadly it takes over your heart!
It makes it beat, faster, harder.
I feel your hands wrapped around me,
You sit behind me, looking into the new horizons.
I am taking you to safety, I am taking you with me!
Pain in the past and crimes against you stand no merit here.
The sandy torrents of hate have no place in my land.
As the sun casts the dark shadows upon the floor,
These will be the only black things in our life,
For my love will shine upon this new world, 24 hours a day!

Sideways

As the Sun sets upon a whispery winter,
Casting rays that reflect upon the snow.

I look sideways, avoiding beauty,
Why? I do not know

      I hear a newborn baby cry,
      A wailing of a miracle

Yet I look sideways, avoiding his stare,
Why? I simply do not care

      I look at the sign, sitting by his feet,
      Homeless and hungry, spare a bite to eat?

      I look sideways, avoiding a begging hand,
      Why? You will never understand

      I look sideways when you talk to me,
      I feel your hands touch my face

Grasp me and make me look
Into your loving eyes

      With a sideways glance back,
      Now there's a surprise!

What a Strange Emotion

Love, what a strange emotion,
Sometimes it reminds me of migrating birds
Heading off into the unknown,
But knowing they will return.
Maybe not the same birds,
But they will return,
No timeframe,
No fixed date,
No certainty.
But return they will.

Love, what a strange emotion,
Reminds me of perfect dreams,
Blissful and fulfilling,
But once gone, once awoken,
A dream was all it was.
Close those eyes,
Wish for it to return,
But it doesn't,
But you know, it was a dream,
Worth dreaming.

An English Spring

It's spring now in the UK,
And the cold winter has gone away.
The leech that hibernated in my heart last winter,
Has not succeeded in making me hateful and bitter!

To be free of winter's savageness,
Has only succeeded in bringing me happiness.
I had built a snow woman
And created out of my mind, perfection!

The cold, dark spells, of winter!
Had preserved her,
But as spring battled hard to regain my soul,
The first drops of water, fell to the soil.

A battle enraged within my heart
Between good and evil witchcraft!
My friends that stood like great oak trees,
Spread their love like a summer breeze!

Spring had arrived,
And all that I believed in had died,
Within winter's bleakest heart, she knew she lied!
The English air and smell of pollen,
Had refreshed that smell, of something rotten!

A Sense of Audience

O' what dreams do wait
Upon the stage so bare?
Starstruck, nerves stand and wait,
Upon eyes that stare!

Butterflies in deadweight flight,
Suck upon your bowel!
For now, is the opening night,
Where even cats do growl.

Blinded by the full beam lights
Stars are all you see.
Grinning egos await your plights
And fall so gracefully.

Violence stems from silence,
Pressure in the dark
A sense of audience,
The show begins to start!

Open Spaces

What   beauty   there   is   in   open   spaces,
Nothing   man-made   about   the   moon's   four   phases.
Barren   trees,   against   the   sapphire   sky,
Echoes   from   a   cuckoo's   cry!
Green   fields   and   wooden   fences,
Casting   shadows,   as   dusk   commences
over   England's   lands,   under   lovers   stars,
Sharing   Nature,   which   is   o u r s .

Flirting in Mirrors

I have a new hobby that makes me smirk,
Although I might act like a jerk,
Flirting in car mirrors is good fun
Although unable to look at their bum.

The cheeky grin and naughty smile,
But not at kids, I'm not a paedophile!
The' phone sign' done with the hand,
Is something we all understand.

'Call me,' and you mouth the numbers,
You feel the grind of the car bumpers.
It's a fantasy you can take home at night,
About those behind you, at the traffic light!

Turning the Iron Compass

Turning the iron compass, from South to North
Bringing my direction back on course
The sharp, jagged, metal point cuts deep into my palms.
As I turn away from the curses and charms,
I feel the muscles bulge in my thighs,
As the harpies taunt me from the skies.

Sirens sing their songs of lust,
But what is beauty without trust?
I push and heave, the compass towards West,
Moving further from all the things that I detest!
The five stages of loss come back with vengeance
Denial! Anger! Bargaining! Depression, then Acceptance.
South was bringing me into the pits of despair,
And past memories I could no longer share.

Cries become distant, birds sing instead,
And the air no longer stinks of the rotting dead.
The scars of chaos I received in those barren lands,
Reflect the pain and blood, I have now on my hands.
Dark days, long nights, a falling descent,
I head North to a place, where I can repent.

My feet hit solid ground and the compass's arrow moves freely,
The pain and the stress leave my body.
The sun comes up from the eastern horizon,
Guiding the compass to a northern direction.
After months and months of turning the compass, I can let go,
And head into the sun and its warm, refreshing glow!

Seagulls In London

How evident that
Your colours mirror
The overcast skies.

No sea here,
Only a river,
Proud and flowing!

Towers of London,
Ravens seek war
In city skies.

Screeching sounds above,
Searching sounds below,
Men, children, birds.

Migration meets integration,
Changing eco-systems,
No Ancient Mariner.

Lost and found,
Hope and prosperity,
Seagulls in London.

Racing Green

All the places my eyes have seen,
And all the places which I've been,
I'm lucky to have lived a dream,
Within the Valleys of Racing Green.

The sunsets and the sunrises,
The unexpected life's surprises,
Within the city, of the tower rises,
Parks of Racing Green are urban disguises.

The road and rail tracks that criss-cross,
Hopes dangle from dental floss,
Like pancakes they freely toss,
Landing in Racing Green coloured moss.

To me, it's a sign of life in death,
A 'something,' when there's nothing left,
A sense of humour, within the jest
Racing Green, at it's best!

For The Kingdom

The drizzle persistently wets the many mouths below,
But it was not water they tasted, but blood!
The frenzy in their eyes would wildly grow,
Mixed with the blood-soaked mud.

Like a sea of sharpened silver spikes,
Not a fingernail between them,
Like machines, they thrust and slash with deadly strikes
Cutting down the fields of men!

The day will be long and rest will not come!
Days may go on until surrender or death is sought!
The battle will go on and on, until someone's won,
And the loser is distraught!

Arrows fly, men charge, shields are lifted!
Like ragdolls they drop, spineless and pale!
Even those who were once gifted,
Clashing of wills, clashes of lives, but to no avail.

The Battle continued as the day dimmed,
Husbands, sons, brothers, torn apart!
Death stank and was carried into the southern wind ,
Screams and sounds of war, go on after dark!

Dawn brings dew, upon the mass of death,
Stragglers are slain and the dead robbed!
But for those who still hear their breath,
Stand silent and pale, and they sobbed!

For victory was theirs, such gallantry,
But what had been won? Land, freedom?
In truth they did not know, they just did their duty,
For God, for Country, for the Kingdom!

Midnight Graffiti

Midnight graffiti upon your door,
Splashed paint stains the floor,
In red crude letters, a belief, not a truth,
Midnight graffiti is now on your roof.

Bird's eye view, in bird shit words,
Full of hate and lies and the absurd.
As the paint dries, so do your tears,
Midnight graffiti spells out your fears.

You're too scared to come out of your home,
Hidden behind curtains, wished to be left alone.
And as the mob gather round,
Midnight graffiti is sprayed on the ground!

And as you wait, the paint finally dries,
But without a trial, you're already tried!
Your guilt lies in whispers and gossip,
As midnight graffiti sprays the latest topic!

Alexander Supertramp

You know how many roads I've crossed?
Junctions gambled?
Trains freeloaded?
Hearts and souls met and embraced?
And yet, I walk alone!

How many hearts I've broken?
And no doubt continue to break.
Thoughts kept and stories told?
And I write this story,
This final chapter, alone.

Into the wild I went,
And the wild went into me,
For what greatness I've known,
What natural beauty I've seen,
'happiness is best, when shared.'

As December Approaches

As December approaches,
A kiss is blown from afar.
How blissful the wind rages,
In these English winter months.
As the year slows down,
Like a car, approaching speed humps,
Coldness in the air and in the breath,
But no coldness in the heart.
Everyone revelling in the festive fun,
And a new year, new start,
The colours of the trees are yellow and brown,
But the sky's still blue,
But whatever the season,
I'm thinking of you.

On Lantern Hill

On Lantern Hill, where the lights do burn,
Amongst the fields of wild growing fern,
White wax drips in it's halls of power,
Upon silhouettes of the castle's tower.
Whispers flutter, behind the walls,
Spread like wildfire, and howling wolves!

Spring brings promise, on the hill,
Harvests grow, like Man's free will.
A symbol stands, tall and proud,
Beneath the village's busy crowd.
Moons rise and Suns set,
Upon a land of no regret.

As the wick burns slowly, but bright,
Giving life in the darkened night,
Shadows stretch, like waking arms,
Spreading sleepy, daybreak charms.
Awake from dreams, they wait their turn,
On Lantern Hill, where the lights do burn.

Do Not Judge A Man

Do not judge a Man
When his soul is broken,
And sorrow, rules his heart.
Where demons dance
Amongst his shadows,
Within a world torn apart!

Do not judge a Man
For his words,
When rage is new to him.
Beliefs enforced upon
His broken dreams,
And the tragedy within.

Do not judge a Man
When at rock bottom
He has come!
His tears engulf him,
Like torrential rain,
Blinded by what he's done.

Judge him now!
As he hands do reach
The tops of the pit above!
Pulling himself out,
Freedom and peace,
Cooing like the dove.

Judge him now,
For his strength,
To battle his inner foe!
Back now straight,
Eyes alert,
His face now all aglow.

Judge him now
For his survival,
To be reborn again.
Learned from his darkened past,
Wise and compassionate,
Cured now from his pain.

For what was once,
Is not now,
His soul, no longer broken,
Is now healed,
And his heart now beats,
A new Man has awoken!
A Man not judged!

The Unfairness Of Angels

No one lives forever, that's a fact,
Not even God's own diplomats.
Goodness and grace,
Never leave your face,
Not even in your resting place
Footprints washed away, without a trace.

What's so fair about greed and hate?
The Unfairness of Angels, a chosen fate!
The illness of this special virtue,
Has now been taken out of you!
Why? No one knows! Not even the creator,
His answering machine says, *'please call back later'*

Many times I've tried to contact him,
He never calls back, he's not listening.
I sit and wait for answers,
How quickly time passes.
I question whether he exists?
You poor Angels, your maker's a sadist!

Why ignore the demons down below?
When they're the ones running the show.
Content with havoc and grief,
They mock our made-up belief!
Whilst we worry what tomorrow brings,
Those Angels endure our sins.

Inside, you feel resentment brew,
As the Angels hide from us what's true
I'm sorry Angel, I only wish I was able,
To uphold your label.
There's nothing my mortal powers can do!
Except to apologise, for the way God's treated you!

We know the way it should have been,
The Eden we should have seen!
Eve was the apple of Adam's eye,
His love made us die.
He betrayed us, so now he betrays you,
Heaven must be his own immortal soul zoo!

Is Heaven so short of good people like yourself?
Does he choose the best for Himself?
Does he look through his window,
Upon his mess, that corrupts below?
Raping our souls and hearts!
Within Earth's amusement parks,

Unfairness, it's all unfair!
There is no God! So beware!
Yet like fools, we stand by him,
This eternal light that shines so dim.
As a race, we're scared of the unexplained,
And repent, when our morals are stained!

Stop looking for questions,
And start making suggestions!
Do we really care what the future brings?
In this world of shortcomings,
The Unfairness of Angels,
Morality, with wings!

The Unity Of Brothers

Like a boa constrictor
Cross bred with an anaconda
That's the strength of the bond
More powerful than a magic wand
A love beyond all others
The unity of brothers

Mithril armour and dragon's scales
Thick blubber from blue whales
Impenetrable is the core
Of such a feeling to explore
A bond made pure by their mother
To each and every special brother

The older one is David, wise and strong
Knows the difference from right and wrong
Steadfast, solid like an oak
But human enough to share a joke
He is the star as dusk covers
The unity of brothers

Ben is the youngest of the three
I'm in the middle you see
Gifted with an actor's charm
He'd never bring you any harm
Gentle, kind, a fine young man
The master with the master plan

Like three pillars of granite stone
They stand never, ever, alone
Unbreakable, immovable
But completely lovable
A love beyond all others
The unity of brothers!

Jocelyn Bartram

It's 2009, the 10th October.
A day for which, I'll always remember,
A day when maybe Angels are fair?
And life isn't all about despair.
Maybe it's fate that this book is late?
A chance to write this final poem,
Because there was no sign of knowing,
That life would come full circle,
And produce life's true miracle.
A baby girl has been born,
Into a family, so tender and warm.
Eternal love has been created,
And boy, have we waited,
For a Bartram girl to come into this world,
Once again, we have excelled,
In creating your memory everlasting.
She has your smile, your eyes and grace,
Your love, your strength, and your face,
What anger was seething within,
The pain and suffering,
The quest for answers, unknowing,
To questions, ongoing.
All answered now, all is clear,
No more darkness, no more fear.
God, whoever he or she may be,
Has now answered me,
The Unfairness of Angels is part of life,
And although it hurts like a twisted knife,
Love conquers all!

I see it in this human so small,
She will grow up with an Angel by her,
To care for, teach and gently guide her
Just like you did for us, Mum,
From the unknown place, you will come,
And breathe through her soul, words unspoken
You have a granddaughter Mum, Jocelyn Bartram.

Printed in the United States
by Baker & Taylor Publisher Services

Printed in the United States
by Baker & Taylor Publisher Services